Coconut Mon

by **LINDA MILSTEIN**
pictures by **CHERYL MUNRO TAYLOR**

TAMBOURINE BOOKS · NEW YORK

Library of Congress Cataloging in Publication Data
Milstein, Linda Breiner. Coconut mon / by Linda Breiner Milstein :
illustrated by Cheryl Munro Taylor. — 1st ed.   p. cm.
Summary: The coconut man sells his ten coconuts one by one.
[1. Coconuts—Fiction. 2. Counting—Fiction. 3. Blacks—Caribbean Area—Fiction.
4. Caribbean Area—Fiction.] I. Taylor, Cheryl Munro, 1957- ill. II. Title.
III. Title: Coconut mon. PZ7.M6646Co 1995 [E]—dc20 94-27171 CIP AC
ISBN 0-688-12862-9. — ISBN 0-688-12863-7
1 3 5 7 9 10 8 6 4 2
First edition

For Rachel and Samantha Rode,
Kimberly Farber,
Andy and Danny Breiner,
Jaclyn, Samantha, and Noah Adelsberg,
and Noah and Zena Milstein

L.M.

For Brooksie

C. M.T.

CO-CO-NUTS!

One dollar buys a coconut!

Come get your coconuts from the Coconut Mon!

COCOnuts!

Eight de-LIC-i-ous

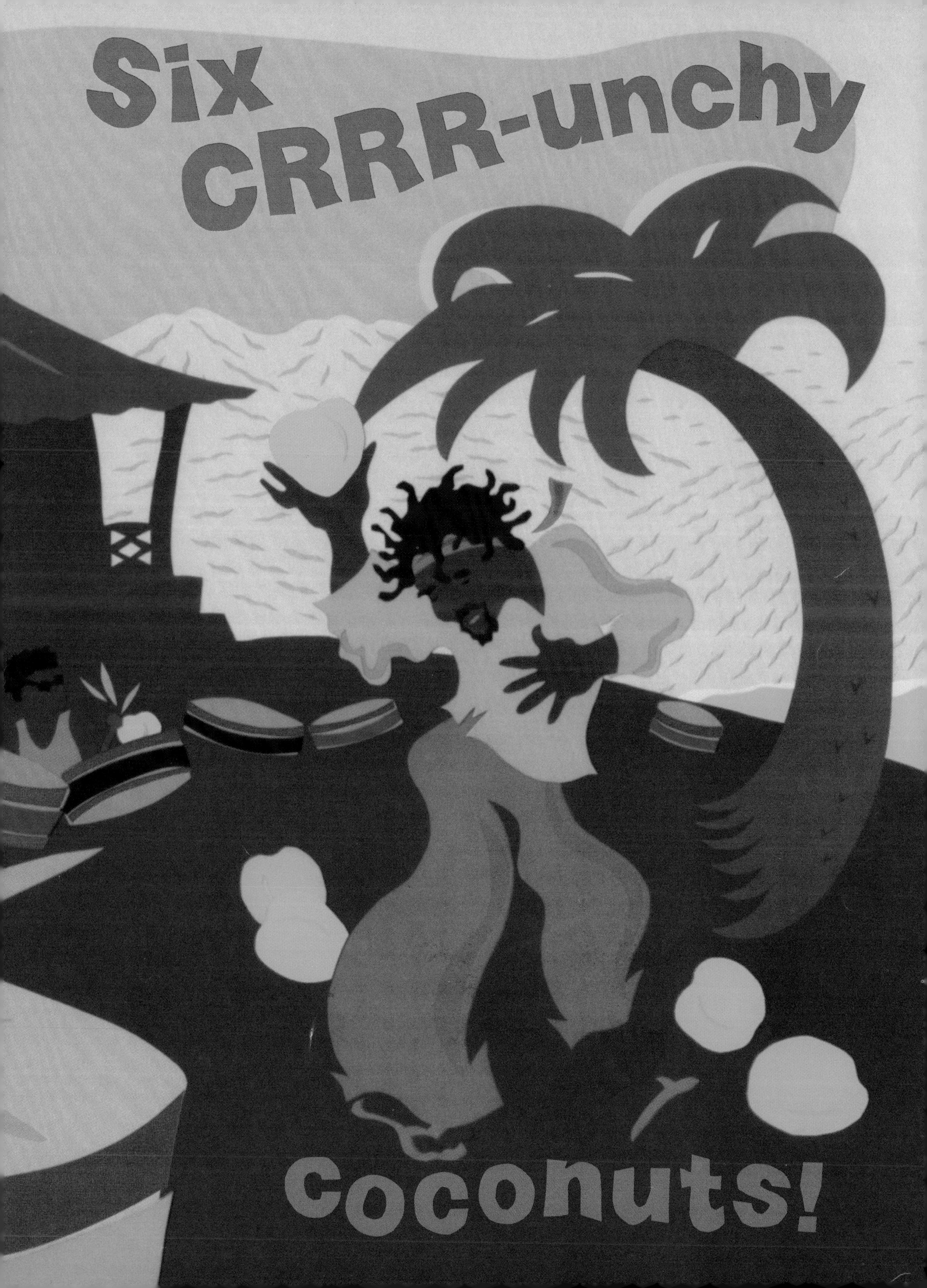
Six
CRRR-unchy
coconuts!

Coconuts!

Get them from the Coconut Mon!

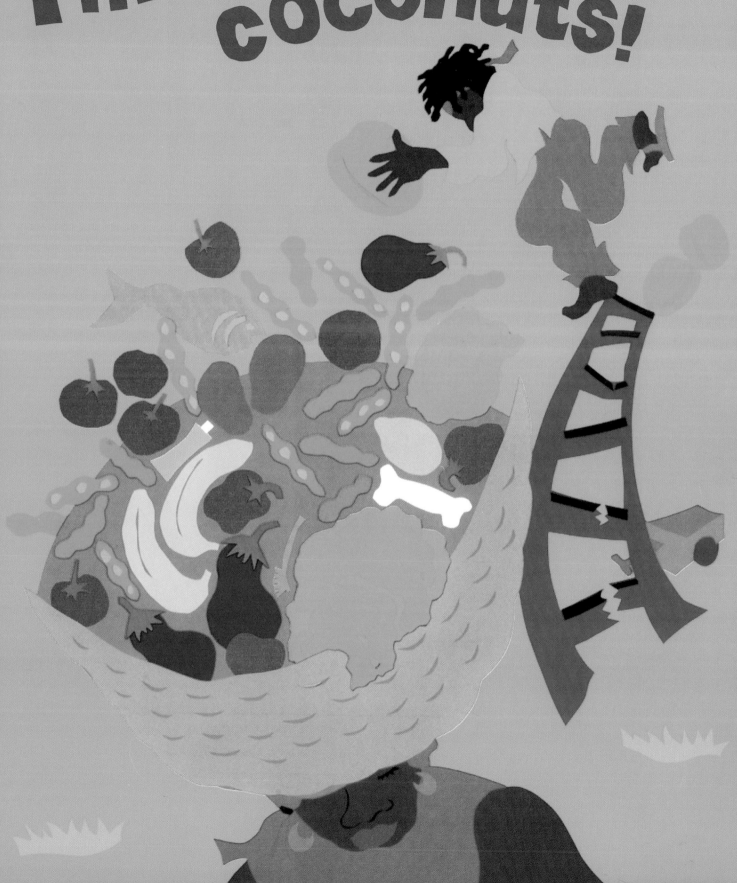

Two SSss-weet coconuts!

Get them from the Coconut Mon!

Do you like sweet
coconut to eat,
young mon?

Take this coconut!
This GOOOOD coconut!

Thank you for
this CO-co-nut,
Mr. Coconut Mon.

CO-CO-NUT!
De-LIC-i-ous coconut!

Come share
my coconut
EV-ER-Y-ONE!

Enough for all
in the hot, HOT sun!